Together atop Sapphire Lookout

a Firehawks Lookout romance story

by

M. L. Buchman

Published by Buchman Bookworks

Discover more by this author at:
www.mlbuchman.com

Cover images:
Fire Lookout © Angela Redmon
Hiker and foxtail pines (Pinus balfouriana)
on John Muir Trail - Pacific Crest Trail ©
Miguel Vieira

Other works by M.L. Buchman

The Night Stalkers

Main Flight

The Night Is Mine
I Own the Dawn
Wait Until Dark
Take Over at Midnight
Light Up the Night
Bring On the Dusk
By Break of Day

White House Holiday

Daniel's Christmas
Frank's Independence Day
Peter's Christmas
Zachary's Christmas
Roy's Independence Day
Cornelia's Christmas

and the Navy

Christmas at Steel Beach
Christmas at Peleliu Cove

5E

Target of the Heart
Target Lock on Love

Firehawks

Main Flight

Pure Heat
Full Blaze
Hot Point

Flash of Fire
Wild Fire

Smokejumpers
Wildfire at Dawn
Wildfire at Larch Creek
Wildfire on the Skagit

Delta Force
Target Engaged
Heart Strike

Angelo's Hearth
Where Dreams are Born
Where Dreams Reside
Maria's Christmas Table
Where Dreams Unfold
Where Dreams Are Written

Eagle Cove
Return to Eagle Cove
Recipe for Eagle Cove
Longing for Eagle Cove
Keepsake for Eagle Cove

Deities Anonymous
Cookbook from Hell: Reheated
Saviors 101

Dead Chef Thrillers
Swap Out!
One Chef!
Two Chef!

SF/F Titles

Nara
Monk's Maze
The Me and Elsie Chronicles

Get a free Starter Library at:
www.mlbuchman.com

1

Danny Chay reached the fire lookout tower in the heart of the Sapphire Mountains and decided that this was about the most crazy-assed thing he'd ever done. Sapphire Mountains sounded like some kinda girly shit, at least until he'd hiked into them. The rugged rock peaks of southwestern Montana jagged upward out of forests so thick that there was no way to see the ground beneath them.

Four months ago he'd never seen more trees than a city park. And the parks in East LA weren't exactly about Mother Nature—more like a quick drug deal or a fast, cheap screw.

Didn't matter what color you were, hanging with the bros was about the only other thing going down.

The view from standing beside Pintler fire lookout tower swept a vast circle in the heart of the Idaho and Montana wilderness. Ten-thousand-foot peaks and dark green forest ran as far as the eye could see in every direction. No hazed gray sky here; it was so blue that it hurt to look up.

He didn't know whether he hated the woman who'd sent him on this damned quest, or if he should kiss her feet. But Kee Stevenson was someone you sure as hell didn't argue with.

She'd rolled back into the neighborhood after most of ten years gone, driving an immaculate, late-model, black Chevy Suburban, kind the Feds drove—which had scared him crapless even though he'd been clean at the time.

The tinted driver's window had slid down and there was Kee.

"Chay."

"Smith. Thought you were dead."

"Stevenson now."

Good as dead. He'd never figured her for the settling down kind.

"You want your shot at getting a life? Get in."

Anyone less dangerous than Kee, he might have tried rolling her for the wheels. Fifty grand on the hoof, ten to fifteen at the chop shop. She was maybe half his size, but if it came down to taking bets in a scuffle, he'd put his money on her.

Danny looked at her, same as ever. Half Asian and half who-knew-'cause-Mama-sure-didn't as she called herself. Serious body totally built to last and the best shot with a handgun he'd ever seen.

He checked the area. No one in obvious sight, but he could feel folks scanning him.

Hey, check out Danny kissing up to the Feds. What's up with that shit?

He could talk that down…not a lot of people dared mess with him, even after Kee bugged out. But that was the point, she'd found a way out. They'd talked about it a lot back in the day. Never seemed possible. When she'd evaporated, he'd assumed the street had swallowed her up.

But Kee never spoke anything but the cold, hard truth. She'd found a way and all these years later had come back to offer it to him.

He got in.

Straight through the night she'd driven in silence, but she'd always been that way, even back when they ran together on the streets. They'd been tight. Not that kind of tight, but the kind where you knew if she had your back there were no worries coming from that direction.

East. She drove way the hell east into the kind of land he'd never seen. Deserts drier than the LA streets during the Santa Ana winds. Places where the next building was fifty miles away.

She'd finally pulled over in nowhere New Mexico desert just after sunrise.

"Out. Your gear is in the back."

"What the f—" But he'd chopped it off when he'd seen her look.

He'd slouched around to the back of the Suburban, popped the rear door, and tried to make sense of what he was looking at. It was a pristine backpack. Not the school books kind for geeks, but one near as big as Kee. Straps sticking out of it in every direction, it was the craziest looking thing he'd ever seen.

She came around and dragged it out, like it was heavy. Held it up while he slid his arms into place, then she let go and he'd nearly hit the ground. It wasn't just heavy, it was like filled with a Chevy straight-six engine block. Before he could complain, she had him strapped in and cinched down.

He half expected her to padlock it on him, but she didn't.

Instead she'd handed him a book: *Hiking the Continental Divide Trail.*

"What the f—"

"You already said that. You're here," she flipped it open to a picture that looked just like the man-tall concrete monument standing twenty feet away in the blazing sun. It was weird, like he was actually in the book. "When you get to the other end," she flipped to the last page to show him, "there's a phone number of a good friend of mine at a place called Henderson's Ranch in Montana."

"This is my magical out? Walking to fucking Montana? Have you totally lost your shit, Kee?"

She'd slammed the back of the Suburban and headed for the driver's door, but stopped the moment before climbing back in.

"You want it, Danny? You've got to prove just how bad you want it. Don't disappoint me." Then she'd slammed the door and was gone in a cloud of dust.

No one had ever believed in him. No one but Kee. He could argue with anything but that last line.

He had staggered up to the trail's entrance sign. It said that the spot was named for a crazy cook who had committed cold-blooded murder on this spot in 1907. He was totally down with that.

A cardboard sign flapping in the dusty breeze read, "Canada, 3,100 miles. Pure Hell, 100 feet."

No shit.

2

Lexi Forrester decided to live up to her name.

“I’m so done with this,” she’d told her business partners.

“You don’t walk away from a successful law firm just two years after making partner.”

“Watch me!” She’d dumped her caseload right there on the conference room table. No longer her problem. How many more times could she stand to face: “My parents never wrote a will.” Or “I want to sue that cheater until he roasts in hell.” Or “I was under mental duress when I pulled that knife in a bar brawl.” Or…

Or nothing. She was done. Law school. The bar. Seven years climbing up the partner track and making it—

She was so done.

If she never saw Boise, Idaho again it would be too soon.

Her best friend, her mom, and her judicial-clerk-sometimes-boyfriend had all protested that she was having a nervous breakdown. Dad was the only one who offered any encouragement, a "just maybe" tilt of his head and shrug while Mom had ranted—or maybe he'd just been cracking his neck. It was always hard to tell with him. She'd been half afraid Mom would have her committed before she could escape.

Lexi had chosen something completely different from anything she'd ever done before. From anyone she'd ever *been* before. It was just one summer, but it was would make a clean break.

She hoped that spending a season working as a fire lookout high in the Sapphire Mountains would let her see what she was going to do next. So far, she wasn't having much luck with that.

3

It** had **been hell. Danny had never appreciated the luxury of a water faucet as much as he had tromping through the New Mexico desert.

He'd quit a hundred nights on the trail, but woken up in the morning and forced himself back into motion. Sometimes it was imagining what the homies would be thinking if they could see him, grunting out another day—not a one of them lame-asses could do this kinda shit.

It took digging deep and those squatters didn't know dingo-crap about that.

Neither had he, but he was learning.

Sometimes it was the thought of Kee kicking his ass if he quit.

No, that wasn't her style. If he quit, she'd leave him in his gutter to die. Which only made him dig in harder.

Eventually though, once he'd gotten over the misery of the daily grind, he'd gotten to noticing the countryside around him. The desert wasn't barren. "Cactus is what grows in the desert," is what he would have said if you'd asked him before. But so did twisted pine trees that offered welcome shade. He saw hares, deer, coyotes, and more types of birds than he'd known existed. At one of the little towns he'd considered grabbing a book about them, but it weighed too much. He might have gotten used to hauling around a Chevy straight-six engine block on his back, but he didn't want to upgrade it to a Ford V-8.

Decent boots were swapped for good ones… he'd found an envelope for expenses stuffed deep in the pack. Along with a list of mail drops. At each drop there'd been a case of food, some emergency shit for blisters and such that he appreciated, and just enough cash to either see him home or on to the next mail drop.

Not a single word from her. He'd known she was a tough bitch—had to be to survive the kind of shit she'd been through even before she bugged out. But he had no idea how tough until he began climbing toward the San Juan Mountains.

There were route choices along the way. By the time he hit the first big one in Colorado, there was no way he was taking the easy path. Screw the Creede cut-off, he punched right up above the tree line—half the nights waking up to find frost on his bag, tromping through late snow during the day.

Nothing had prepared him for the plains of central Wyoming, the crazy steep Tetons, or the wonders of Yellowstone.

A lot of alone time out on the trail. Vast amounts of it. He'd hiked for a week with a very giving and seriously well-built woman named Crissy through a section of Colorado. He'd promised to stay in touch though they both knew he never would. But he'd seen less people in three months than he'd see in a typical LA afternoon.

Somehow, the whole thing caught up with him as he climbed up the trail to Pintler fire lookout in the southwest corner of Montana—his last state, the brutal Idaho Bitterroots thankfully behind him.

4

Mid-summer was mostly gone from her eagle's aerie atop the Continental Divide, eight thousand feet up in the Sapphires. Lexi hadn't made any progress toward what came after the fire lookout job, but she wouldn't trade this summer in for the world.

She'd made radio friends with other lookouts and spotted her fair share of forest fires, but mostly, she'd had nothing but the wilderness and time.

Oh, she'd ridden through all of the ups and downs they'd warned her about. Horror at the choices she'd made in burning her bridges in the Boise legal community. Wondering if she'd lost her mind to make this crazy choice in the first place. Depression that she was having a mid-life crisis before her thirtieth birthday—she'd always been an overachiever, but this one she could have done without.

But she'd also slowly regained some form of inner equilibrium, something she'd lost a long time ago. She'd taken to rising with the sun and going for fast hikes and eventually mountain runs before her nine a.m. spotter duties began. She'd been track-and-field in high school, especially the shorter distances. The fast, brutal sprint—the high adrenaline of both the challenge and the victory—had fit her like a glove. Now she discovered the attraction of the longer runs, letting nature just sweep by as she ran through trees, past lakes, and over hills.

Lexi knew reality would come crashing back through her front gate in another couple months, but she was going to avoid it as long as she could.

On the radio she'd made the day's final "no smoke" call except for the fire still being fought on West Goat Mountain—one of hers.

Chatted for a few minutes with Patty who said the wolf pack she was following had veered north, so no visit this time—bad news for Lexi and for Patty's husband up at Gray Wolf Summit lookout. Tess and Marta were trading recipes. Signing off, Lexi took a mug of tea and went to sit on her lookout tower's verandah to admire the sunset. Verandah, fancy word for the narrow wooden service walkway around the outside of the small cab that was her home.

The sky was just shifting from blue to gold when she heard the happy sigh of someone sloughing off their pack at the campsite below. She'd learned to recognize a lot by that sound. Pintler Lookout lay directly on the Continental Divide Trail, and its high peak always seemed to be the end of a hiker's day.

Some were short-section hikers, taking a week or two summer's vacation to do a stretch. Their groans were far more heartfelt, often accompanied by hisses of pain. But once settled, they were a generally cheery group, teasing each other good naturedly about their next vacation being in Hawaii.

In early summer, the ones hiking the trail from north to south—Canada to Mexico—had six hundred miles under their belts by the time they reached her. Grumbling and discouragement were common: not yet through the first of the five states on the route most found to be brutally depressing. She'd taken to avoiding them when she could, hiding two stories above in her tower. It was amazing how few of that type climbed the last sets of stairs to admire the view. The last of the "sobos," the south-bound through-hikers, had dwindled out by July. Any later and they'd get caught in the snowy peaks in Colorado.

This time the sigh was different and she leaned over the railing to see why.

5

"Pintler Lookout," Danny said it aloud to hear his own voice in the vast silence. The only other noises were the rustling of a soft breeze through the low grass and a bald eagle crying somewhere far above.

The silence, which had creeped the shit out of him even more than the scorpions and rattlesnakes those first few weeks, was now an easy place to be. Even the memory of East LA noise, the car horns, the sirens, the hard laughter...all of it made him wince.

Had that been Kee's plan? Ruin his past by giving him a new view? If so, it had sure as hell worked. He'd given up wondering about that phone number on the last page of the trail guide. Whatever the future held for him, didn't matter. For now he was down with the moment. Getting through each day. Seeing what it would bring. Wasn't a soul in his old neighborhood that had seen shit like this view or breathed air this clean.

He dumped his pack but stayed standing, shaking out the familiar buzz in his legs. That was another thing they'd never believe back home. Walking over two thousand miles, he was strong enough now to squish any ten of his pals. He'd had to buy new jeans and shirts twice on the trip because they'd gotten too tight.

"Hi," a voice floated to him through the still air.

For a second he thought he'd imagined it.

"Where you in from?"

He looked around, but he was the only one here. "Uh, New Mexico."

"My first nobo," the voice was very soft, unaccented, female. Had he suddenly lost his mind? It was like the mountaintop was asking him questions. "Straight through?"

"Uh-huh. Twenty-three hundred miles or some such, so far."

"Ahead of the whole pack."

Danny hadn't known that, but liked it just fine. He'd dusted any number of folks on the trail, once he got his feet under him. Not a single north-bound through-hiker ahead of him. That explained why the trail had been so lonely. He'd camp with sobos for a night or north-bound section hikers for a couple days to a week, but mostly it had been him and the trail.

"By yourself?" This time he caught the direction of the voice and looked up. A face was peering down at him over the railing on the lookout tower. A bright smile and a mop of bright red hair turned dark copper by the golden light of the sky behind her.

"Solo," he confirmed. "You?" Then knew that wasn't the best question to ask a single woman in the wilderness.

"I'm manning the lookout this summer," a slight evasion, but not much.

"Nope," he sat down on his pack so that he'd look less threatening and turned back to the sunset.

"What do you mean, 'nope'?" The woman on high sounded confused.

"I figure you're womanning the lookout this summer."

That earned him a sparkling laugh that did funny things inside him. There was nothing fake about it. It wasn't the laugh of someone wanting something or cozying up to him trying to be casual, pretending that there wasn't about to be some kind of deal going down. It wasn't a laugh by some buddy because you'd cracked a dirty joke, no matter how lame, and the laugh was expected. Hers just spilled out into the sky.

Her light tread sounded across the platform over his head and down the stairs.

"Thanks," she said as she came to stand beside him. "I've been trying to figure out what I was doing here all summer. Now I know."

Danny scoffed, "Damn if that ain't a feeling I know. Don't suppose you can tell me what I'm doing on this hike? I'm doin' it, just still not sure why." Her silhouette was enough to tell him lean and fine. In jeans and a t-shirt she looked classy. Maybe the way she carried herself so straight.

"Nope," she admitted cheerfully. "Unless your 'manning' it."

Something about that was too accurate to keep inside and a laugh just burst out of him, echoing off the night.

Her bright laugh joined his deep one for a moment.

"You've got no idea, sister. Christ you have no idea." That's exactly what Kee had done to him—forced him to man up rather than slumming through life. It was like the core of the whole thing: this hike, his life. It was about time he took ownership of it.

"Danny Chay," he held out a hand. "From… shit, I don't even know anymore. From the Continental Divide Trail I guess." He sure couldn't see himself back in East LA.

6

"Leanna Forrester, but everyone calls me Lexi." She took his hand and shook it. Normally she would have hesitated, especially with a guy who was so much bigger than she was. His hand completely enveloped hers. Normally she'd have had her can of bear-repelling mace in her other hand. But something about that contented sigh and his deep easy laugh had made her feel safe. No, it had made her feel welcome. Welcome on her own mountaintop, welcome in her own life.

"From," and then the joke slammed into her. She did her best to lower her voice and imitate his tone, “From…shit, I don’t even know anymore. Top of the Sapphire Mountains I guess.” Then the laugh burst out of her, bordering way to close to a choke.

“Better sit down before you fall down, woman.” He moved over to a handy rock and waved for her to sit on his softer pack which was awfully decent of him. Her knees did give out a bit, dropping her down onto the pack.

“I think I just sat on your cooking pot,” she shifted to a more comfortable position.

“Couldn’t hurt the damned thing anyway.”

His tone, his use of language—she’d only heard it in the movies, street punk grown man tall. A storm of nerves slammed into her and she clamped her arms together against the sudden chill. Should she get up? Would he let her?

But Danny did nothing but look back out at the evening. One she was sure that’s all he was going to do, she did the same. Pintler was a promontory that fell away steeply to the east and west and was nearly a cliff to the south. The trail wound in from the northwest and departed to the northeast. The sunset turned the hundred peaks and the hundred thousand trees into a tapestry of gold-tinted pinnacles rising from the green-black hills and valleys far below. The last of the swallows still skittered across the sky, the bats weren't out yet.

"First star," he pointed west.

It took her a moment to spot it. "That's Venus."

"First planet," he said in exactly the same way, pointing again as if he'd just noticed it.

And once more she felt more desire to smile than to be afraid.

He was looking around the sky, apparently searching for the next one to reveal itself. It would be Jupiter to the southeast, but not for another ten or fifteen minutes.

"Are you a good man, Danny?" Now there was a dumb question. Like a bad one would tell the truth.

He glanced at her, then rubbed a hand across his chin. Clean-shaven, unlike most who hiked the trail. His hair was long, down to his collar, but had looked clean while she could still see it. It had looked nice on him, a little wild, a little dangerous, though not in a bad way.

Not her type at all. In fact…

"A good man," he said it flat. "The way I'm guessing you mean it, sister, not very."

Her nerves slammed back in full force.

"But maybe," he turned back to searching the sky. "Just maybe, I'm slowly haulin' my ass there."

7

Normally Danny slept the sleep of the trail hiker—lie down and crash hard. At least once he'd gotten over the vast silence of the night, and the startling tiny noises of different creatures.

Lying beside the lookout tower, staring up at the underside of the decking, knowing that Lexi was sleeping right there, sleep had eluded him.

They'd talked a long time. More than he'd talked to anyone out on the trail, and about deeper shit than he'd talked about with anyone, maybe ever.

Not the past. That was so far away he barely remembered it anymore.

She hadn't either.

It was like they were both born at the start of this summer. He'd told her about Kee, but it was like his life had started the moment he climbed into that Suburban. Just "friend from my past came and hauled my ass to New Mexico." Nothing more.

They hadn't talked about the future either. Just the summer: his long hike, her long vigil.

When she'd finally stood, shivering with the chill night air, and wished him goodnight, she'd done one thing more.

She'd rested on of those fine hands upon his shoulder and kissed him atop the head.

"That thing about you becoming a good man, Danny? Sounds like you're already there." Then she'd been gone. At least from beside him, if not from his thoughts.

The next morning he woke to the sound of her tread descending the tower's wooden stairs. The unnaturalness of the sound dragged him up from his brief sleep.

She waved at him, then turned and ran off into the woods.

It was all he could do to wave back. He'd barely seen her the night before. Now in the bright light, he'd gotten an eyeful. She was tall, maybe most as tall as he was. Her brilliant red hair cascaded and curled down to her shoulders. Lexi was as fine as a willow branch…he knew what those looked like now. Her shorts revealed long runner's legs and her t-shirt revealed not one extra ounce anywhere.

He couldn't believe that she was alone in the woods. Why he'd smack her upside the head for being so damn stupid that…

Then he got to thinking about it, looking out at the vast wilderness. A woman, even one who looked that good, was probably far safer here than back in LA. She wouldn't last a minute on his streets. There was too much fresh air and innocence about her.

Innocence wasn't right either. She'd clearly seen some shit. Not his kind of shit, but enough to make her pretty disappointed in the world.

But there was lightness about her. He could still hear her bright laugh. It had made him tell his hardest, blackest moments of the hike in such a way as to get her to let loose that laugh some more. And she'd done the same. He could feel her doing it, as they'd sat on pack and rock near enough to whisper, digging deep into the internal shitheap and reforging it in the night.

He'd planned to just overnight here. Thought about it some more. It might be best if he did go, maybe best for both of them. He'd just go up and check out the view from the tower, pack up, and get out. He unpacked the stove that had given him so much trouble at first, and started oatmeal in his bent cooking pot. Yanking and tugging on it didn't quite fix the damage done by Lexi's fine ass, but it was good enough for oatmeal.

More time with the leggy Lexi Forrester might give his needs a hard time, though he knew to keep his hands to himself until she offered. But he wasn't sure he wanted to break the shitbubble of his past and spill it out for her to see.

Four months ago, he'd been proud of that past. He had massive street cred. Not only was he a survivor, but he understood the power that came from protecting people, even from themselves. He was the one who talked them out of the stupidest plans, or at least tried to.

He was the one who made a point of visiting his buddies in the slammer when they hadn't listened.

Talking to Lexi last night, going deep inside, he'd begun to understand how small his world had been. He'd become better than all that. It was the unknown future that was now scaring the crap out of him.

"You're thinking awfully hard there, Danny," Lexi gasped out from close beside him.

He looked up at her. Shaking out her arms and legs. Her chest heaving behind her thin t-shirt. Damn! He was as much of a breast man as the next guy, but who ever knew that compact could look so good. Forcing himself not to stare, he looked up at her workout-charged smile shining on her ever-so-white face. Freckles enough to be damned cute without enough to make her look childish. She was pure woman, and that was before he got to her dazzling blue eyes—darker, richer than should be possible.

"Thinking about the future shit I *don't* know," he managed. And thinking about the woman he'd like to.

"Don't go there."

He wondered which thought she was talking about.

"Every time I think about what happens at the end of fire season, it scares the pee out of me."

He was down with that.

"Bring your breakfast up when it's ready. I just need a minute for a washcloth shower and a change of clothes."

Now there was an image he was *totally* down with.

8

Lexi had her own oatmeal with raisins started before she felt the vibration of Danny's heavy tread climbing the tower. She waved him into the cab—the fourteen-foot-square room that was her home. It had a counter along two walls that was her work area, kitchen, and small library. Two chairs took another wall, and a cot and the door took the fourth. The center was dominated by the large circle of the Osborne fire finder—the lookout's main tool for mapping a fire's location once it had been spotted.

While she'd been waiting for him, she'd

done another inspection of the surrounding hills, even though it wasn't time yet. The West Goat fire was smaller than it had been last night, the ground teams must have worked right around the clock. Nothing else new. It was either inspect the forest or go through some pointless straightening and cleaning routine for her visitor.

She turned to face him and took a step back into the Osborne. Lexi hadn't seen him standing up before. She was almost six foot, he had to duck to make sure he didn't bang his head on the door. So at least six three. And wide enough of shoulder that she was surprised he didn't have to turn sideways to step through. The cab suddenly felt tiny and claustrophobic despite the big windows that wrapped all the way around.

His heritage looked mixed, giving him darker skin than hers, which was true for everyone on the planet. But it was light enough that she could see the deep tan from his living outdoors for the last several months. Black hair, dark eyes, but he didn't feel dangerous.

"If I'm making you nervous…" he gestured toward the door with his bowl.

"No," she couldn't be nervous around him after last night's discussions. No one had ever spoken to her that way, laying out such deep truth. And, for the first time, it had made her do the same…something she definitely wasn't used to in herself. Even her internal dialog never did that. She'd simply been sick to death of lawyering and decided it was time for a change.

Danny really thought about things… about shit. She almost giggled at her own Dannyism.

"No, not nervous. At least not in a bad way," and she knew exactly what sleepless thoughts that had come from. "Just a little surprised at how big…" and there was no way to finish that sentence that would be in any manner seemly.

He waited a beat then filled the small cab with his deep, reverberating laugh. He made an Incredible Hulk-like motion, holding out his arms and pushing out his chest.

"You're going to spill your breakfast."

That deflated him as he re-angled his bowl in time to save his oatmeal.

She'd never met a man who laughed at himself so easily. Or who let her do the same.

9

Danny was torn between which view to admire: the landscape or the woman. All morning, with an interruption every thirty minutes for her fire scan, they'd chatted. Not the heavy talk of last night, but easy chatter of the day.

She talked about running.

He about weight-lifting.

High school came up, but they kept it about the people when it became obvious that the two schools were different beyond imagining.

She knew her parents; loved them despite their flaws.

He vaguely remembered his mom before she OD'd, and kept that to himself.

A spaghetti dinner, he donated the pasta and she the sauce, had been about movies. He'd read some books, but nothing like she did. She pulled a battered copy of *The Bourne Identity* off her little shelf and handed it to him.

"Already saw it," he tried to hand it back. He hadn't even known it was a book.

"Trust me," she pushed it back.

And he did.

Sunset after her last sign-off had been spent out on the narrow porch. No room for chairs, just enough to clean the windows…or sit with their backs against the cab and their feet dangling off the edge, out beneath the lowest rail.

They didn't go deep like they had last night, instead they went quiet.

After four months, most of it alone, Danny thought he knew all the forms of quiet. But sitting shoulder-to-shoulder with Lexi Forrester, their tea mugs long since set aside empty, was something new. There was a depth, a texture, a…

For the first time in his life, he wished he

had better words to describe things. Though he'd wager that all of the words in the world wouldn't let him describe Lexi even half what she deserved.

When she rose silently to her feet, he figured it was time to go. But when they reached the small landing between the stairs and the cab's door, she took his hand and tugged him through the door.

He didn't ask, for fear that she'd change her mind if he did.

She didn't say a word. Not then. Not when he took her in the silent darkness, just glad that she had protection because his was some impossible distance away in the pack at the base of the tower. And not when finally spent, she lay down upon his chest and held him.

Sex with Colorado Crissy had always been fast and hard. Almost like an echo of the street in East LA.

Lexi was like the mountains: fresh, full of surprises, and taking the long slow climb up with all the ease of a sunny day's hike. No one had ever given to him that way, shown him what was possible.

He'd expected the morning to be shy and

awkward, so he'd held her close through the night, figuring he'd have to leave soon after daybreak.

Instead she woke the sun and ran a soft hand over his bare chest.

Her first words were, "Can you stay a while?"

Not yeah, but hell yeah.

10

"You have to go!" It was going to kill her if he did, but she knew it was true. Somehow the summer had moved along and not touched them.

Danny looked up at her like she was ripping out his guts. The dawn light was just bright enough that she could see the pain as he lay on their narrow cot—after all these weeks it wasn't hers anymore, it was theirs.

"You know I'm right. The last of the nobo hikers are already racing through; you've seen them hurrying to beat the weather. After walking way over two thousand miles, quitting now with just six hundred to go…you'll never forgive yourself."

"I leave you and I'll never forgive myself!" His snarl appeared to surprise him as much as it did her.

She laid her forehead against his chest, his wonderful chest, and hid there. For an entire glorious August, they had lived in their mountaintop idyll. They'd only come down off the mountain once, a long hike out and back to restock supplies, the substitute lookout coming up for two days for that purpose.

Lexi was so completely gone on him that she couldn't stand it. If the future didn't hold Danny Chay in it, she didn't know what she'd do. Would he fall into the arms of some other lookout-tower babe or some trail-bait? She couldn't imagine it. Didn't want to risk it. But still she knew…

Danny began cursing. A long, effusive string of bitter anger. She was going to miss that. She was going to miss him reading aloud to her every chance they had. She was going to miss the incredible sex and the gift of lying in his arms. She was…

Going to make herself stark raving mad.

"It's not like I'm going anywhere," she managed.

"Neither am I, god dammit!" But she could hear now that he understood he had to go while there was still time—before the winter snows closed the northern trail. He just wasn't ready to accept it yet.

"You'll finish the hike and then you'll come back to me," she did her best to say it so that they'd both believe it.

"Said I wasn't going," though it was hardly even a snarl.

Crap! She was even going to miss his moods.

"I never was real good about staying in touch with women."

That jolted her upright, "But you are this time or I'll kick your ass!"

"Like to see you try, Lexi." That smile that he brought out when he was teasing her shown in the early morning light.

She leaned back down and kissed him hard, running her hands over his body until he groaned with his need for her. If it was even half the need she had for him, he had to come back. He just had to.

11

Six weeks without a word.

Lexi cleaned the windows of the cab one last time before re-hanging the heavy wooden shutters. The fire season was over. The first flurries had already painted the peaks white and the Forest Service was calling all of the lookouts back down. She didn't know where to go or what to do. So she took it by the minute rather than the day, ignoring the tears that kept blurring her vision.

Her pack was full. No garbage left behind. She'd bagged the books she'd brought in Ziplocs so that they'd survive the winter for the next lookout. She took only the Bourne books because Danny had loved them so. She could even hear them now, read out in his deep warm voice.

Danny Chay and Jason Bourne, both men on a path to discovering their true identity. The irony of that only caught up with her now and it made her cry even more than she already was. He was out there somewhere doing just that…she was the one who was completely lost.

She padlocked the door and descended the stairs a final time. The Forest Service asked if she'd be back next summer. Unable to imagine how she could ever come back to all of these memories, she'd refused. Next summer was too far away to think about anyway.

Next season…Crap!

The next hour was almost too much.

She couldn't even look at the tower as she walked away from it.

For three hours she descended the trail, hiking down into misery.

When she reached her Subaru Forester—"Lexi and Subaru Forester," how sad was that as a life's statement—and circled to the rear to stow her pack, the sight that awaited her didn't make any sense. She dumped her pack on the ground.

A big pack was already leaning against the Subaru's rear bumper. A pack that she knew because it had sat in the corner of her tower cab for a month. More battered. Snow crampons and an ice axe tied onto it, but still the same pack.

She spun around desperately searching… and saw Danny sitting on a fallen tree close beside the forest road.

Lexi didn't walk, she flew. Her landing carried him backward right over the log and onto the forest floor covered in fall leaves and deep pine needles.

He held her tight while she wept anew. It was all she could do. Nothing had ever been so big in her life and she simply couldn't hold it inside.

"You made it!" The first words she was able to gasp out.

"Mexico to Canada." By his tone she could hear how doing that had changed him. Made him more complete.

No, it had shown him that he was as complete as she'd already known he was.

He climbed back up on the log and settled her in his lap but she couldn't stop her hands from running over him.

"You're here. You're really here."

"Surprised the shit out of me too," he teased. "But after that place called Pintler Lookout, I could only think about one thing." He kissed her nose and she just leaned into him.

He told her about the rest of the hike, running into the high snows, but buying the gear and going for it anyway. Then hitching a ride back across Montana, rushing to get to her before she came off the mountain.

"I wanted to meet you up above," he pointed at the trailhead to the lookout, "but the Ranger station said you were coming down today. Didn't want to somehow miss you in the woods. Longest damned wait of my life."

She nodded. It was all she had in her.

"I called that number in the back of the trail book."

They'd both puzzled at that final instruction from his enigmatic friend Kee.

"Open invite for both of us if we want to see what the hell winter is like working on a Montana ranch."

Again she nodded, mute with the wonder of the word "we."

"One catch though."

She looked at him and waited. Instead of the teasing smile, he looked nervous. Lexi didn't know of a whole lot of things that could make Danny Chay nervous. When he didn't speak, she slid out of his lap and onto the log to sit beside him.

"Turns out there's a reason other than the incredible color of your eyes that these are called the Sapphire Mountains." Then he nodded down.

In his hands was a small velvet box. In the center of it was a silver ring with a single, brilliant blue sapphire mounted on it.

"It's not much, but it's all I could scrape together. I wanted to get you—"

"Shut up, Danny."

He looked at her in hurt surprise.

"Just shut up. If you say one more thing about something so perfect, I'll kick your ass."

He grinned at that. "Like to see you try, Lexi."

"I absolutely will." The laughter built inside her. She didn't know whether to look at the amazing ring or the incredible man offering it to her. "But first—"

"But first?" He frowned at her, the worry back.

"First you better kneel down properly, propose, and then put that ring on my finger like a really good man should."

And he did just that. Her incredible man who had hiked to her out of the wilderness, knelt before her, and, at a complete loss for words, used his eyes to beg her to be his wife.

Unable to speak herself, she just nodded and held out her hand.

He slid it on her finger and like a miracle, the future wasn't dark or scary. It was as bright as sunlight on a mountaintop.

When he finally stood once more before her, she noted that the log on which they'd been sitting was close behind his knees.

He reached for her.

She shoved hard against his chest and he toppled once more onto the soft leaf and pine.

He managed to snag her hand as he went down and she happily followed him all the way.

About the Author

M. L. Buchman has over 50 novels and 30 short stories in print. Military romantic suspense titles from both his Night Stalker and Firehawks series have been named Booklist "Top 10 of the Year," placing two titles on their "Top 101 Romances of the Last 10 Years" list. His Delta Force series opener, *Target Engaged,* was a 2016 RITA nominee. In addition to romance, he also writes thrillers, fantasy, and science fiction.

In among his career as a corporate project manager he has: rebuilt and single-handed a fifty-foot sailboat, both flown and jumped out of airplanes, and designed and built two houses. Somewhere along the way he also bicycled solo around the world.

He is now making his living as a full-time writer on the Oregon Coast with his beloved wife and is constantly amazed at what you can do with a degree in Geophysics. You may keep up with his writing and receive a free 4-novel starter e-library by subscribing to his newsletter at:

www.mlbuchman.com.

Wild Fire (excerpt)
-the riveting conclusion to the Firehawks series-

"Gordon. Hit the hotspot at your two o'clock."

"*Perfect,*" Gordon Finchley mumbled to himself. The call came from Mark Henderson, the Incident Commander-Air, the moment after Gordon carved his MD 530 helicopter the other way toward a flaming hotspot at eleven o'clock and hit the release on his load of water.

Two hundred gallons spilled down out of his helo's belly tank and punched the cluster of burning alders square in the heart. He glanced back as he continued his turn and the flames were now hidden in the cloud of steam, which meant it was a good hit.

"Die, you dog!" He yelled it at the flames like…Austin Powers…yelling at something. He really had to work on his macho. Or maybe just give it up as a lost cause.

"I have the other one, Mark," Vanessa called up to the ICA from her own MD 530. Her touch of an Italian accent still completely slayed Gordon…and any other guy who met her. Because her "Italian" was more than just her voice.

Gordon twisted his bird enough sideways to watch her, which was always a pleasure, in the air or on the ground. Vanessa Donatella flew her tiny, four-seater helicopter the same way she looked: smooth, beautiful, and just a little bit delicate. Her water attack was also dead on. It punched down the second spot fire, which had been ignited by an ember cast far ahead of the main fire.

The two of them were fighting their aerial battle beyond the head of the wildfire—he and Vanessa were making sure that nothing sparked to life ahead of the line of defense. He could just make out the Mount Hood Aviation smokejumpers suited up in flame-resistant yellow Nomex, defending a ridgeline. The heavy hitters of the main airshow, MHA's three Firehawks and a Twin 212 helicopter, were attacking the primary fire, ducking in and around the columns of smoke and flame to deliver their loads where the smokejumpers most needed them.

He twisted back to straight flight, popped up high enough to clear the leading edge of the flames, then ducked through the thin veil of smoke and dove down over the burning bank at the lake's shore. He could feel the wash of radiated heat through the large windshield that gave him such a great view—a nearly unbroken sweep of acrylic starting below his feet on the rudder pedals, then sweeping above his head. It became much cooler once he punched out over the open lake.

Gordon slid to a hover with his skids just ten feet over the water—low enough to unreel his snorkel hose and let the pump head dip below the lake's surface. It would be forty seconds until he had two hundred more gallons aboard.

Vanessa slid her helo down close beside him and dunked her own hose.

Their helos were identical except for the large identifying numbers on the side. The MD 530 was as small as a helicopter could be and still have four seats. Last season they'd switched from dipping buckets dangling on longlines to belly tanks attached between the skids. There was an art to steering the swinging buckets to their target that Gordon could get nostalgic about, but the tank was certainly more convenient.

Their helos were painted with the MHA colors: gloss black with red-and-orange flames running down the sides. The effect was a bit ruined by the big windshields that made up the whole nose of the aircraft, but Gordon would take the visibility any day.

"Nice hit," he offered. The pilots kept a second radio tuned to a private frequency so that they could coordinate among themselves without interfering with the ICA's commands to the airshow. It also allowed them to chat in these brief quiet moments. In the background was a third radio tuned to the ground team. Thankfully, there weren't any fixed-wing aircraft attacking the fire or there'd be a fourth radio running. When flying solo, it could be harder to fight the radios than the fire.

"You too. It is such a pity that you hit the wrong fire." He could feel Vanessa's warmth in her tease.

"Even a couple seconds more warning would have worked. If I didn't know better, I'd think Mark was doing it on purpose."

"Whine. Whine. Whine."

They shared a smile across the hundred feet that separated them. It was a real bummer that it hadn't worked out between them. After months of silent but—he eventually discovered—mutual attraction, they'd gotten together. Only to have nothing come of it. Making love to someone as beautiful and gentle as Vanessa was a joy, but there'd been no spark. They'd talked about it, tried again, and still nothing. Despite his typical awkwardness around stunning women (most women really) and Vanessa's natural shyness—or perhaps because of the combination—they'd come out of it as close friends. Friends without benefits, which was still a pity, but good friends.

His water tank gauge reached full and he lifted aloft as he reeled in his hose. Vanessa would be about ten seconds behind him.

Together they flew over the flaming bank that sloped steeply up from the lake. No point in fighting that fire, it would burn down to the shore and then there would be nowhere else for it to go. It was simply one flank of the main fire. The head itself was a long burn running south toward a community of homes at the other end of the lake—*that* they had to defend.

Henderson gave him enough lead time to pick his path this time. His whine to Vanessa had some basis. Messing with a pilot didn't sound like Henderson at all, but lately there'd definitely been something going on.

Gordon shrugged to himself.

He was never big on worrying about what came next. After three years of flying for the man, Gordon knew that whatever Henderson's game was, it would show up only when he was good and ready to reveal it. But another part of him—the one that had told his father precisely where he could ram a hot branding iron the day he'd left the family ranch for the last time—decided that if Henderson kept it up, Gordon might need to buy a branding iron of his own.

For now, only the fire mattered. It was getting even more aggressive and it took a punch from both of their birds to kill the next flare-up.

"I'm headed back to base for fuel," Vanessa announced on the command frequency.

"Roger," Henderson called down from his spotter plane three thousand feet above the fire. "Gordon, fly twice as fast."

Typical. "Sure thing, boss man." He flipped a finger aloft, then wiggled his cyclic control side to side to wave at Vanessa by rocking his helicopter. She returned the gesture and peeled off to the northwest. By pure chance, this fire was less than a ten-minute flight from MHA's base on the eastern foothills of Mt. Hood. The eleven-thousand-foot volcanic mountain was a shining beacon of glaringly bright glaciers, even in late September. The midmorning sun was blinding off the high slopes. In moments, Vanessa was a black dot against that white background. She'd be back in under half an hour and then it would be his turn.

Below him was a land of brown and green, heavy on the brown. Eastern Oregon had none of the green lushness that everyone associated with the Oregon Coast and the Willamette Valley. Out here, Ponderosa pine grew far enough apart for grass to grow tall between them. And now, late in the season, the grass was all dried to a dark gold and carried fire fast and hard. The pine and western juniper weren't in much better shape. Several seasons of drought had taken their toll. The hundred-foot grand firs and the fifty-foot alder were all as dry as bone and lit off like Roman candles.

Gordon climbed an extra fifty feet, crossing the worst of it. He remembered back in his rookie year with MHA when Jeannie had a tree blow up directly under her. The superheated sap had cooked off and sent a big chunk of treetop an extra hundred feet aloft. It had knocked out her rear rotor over the New Tillamook Burn Fire. She'd managed to find a clearing the same size as her helo's rotor blades and somehow set down safely in it. Gordon had seen it and still wasn't sure how she'd stuck that landing.

He kept up the hustle: lake, climb over fire, hit the latest flare-up, climb back over, and dive down for more water. Occasionally one of the big helos would be tanking at the same moment he was. He'd always liked his little MD. The Firehawks—the firefighting version of the Black Hawk helicopters—could carry a thousand gallons to his two hundred, and they were damn fast in flight, but they had none of the finesse of his MD. They didn't get up close and personal with the fire. They flew higher and could knock crown fires out of trees. He flew lower and could put out your campfire without messing up the rest of the campsite… well, not too much.

He harassed his best friend Mickey at one point in his Twin 212 as they tankered together. Two-twelves were midsized helos, halfway between his own MD and the big Firehawks—the modern version of the Vietnam-era UH-1 Hueys. It made for a good spread of capabilities on the team, but it didn't mean he had to let Mickey fly easy just because of that.

"Hey buddy, you actually getting any work done?"

"More than you, Finchley."

"Believe that when I see it. Honeymoon over yet?"

"Not even close!" Mickey sounded pretty damned pleased.

"You better be saying that, hubbie" Robin cut in as she hovered her big Firehawk *Oh-one* down over the water.

Gordon was glad for Mickey. His easygoing friend had fallen for Robin, the brash, hard-edged blonde, the moment she'd hit camp at the beginning of the year. They were an unlikely couple from the outside, but it looked like it was working for them. They'd hooked up on day one, married last month, and showed no signs of the heat easing—of course, anything involving Robin Harrow would be fiery hot. Gordon wasn't jealous, he really wasn't. MHA's lead pilot was a primal force and would have run right over any lesser man than Mickey. Way too out there for Gordon. The quiet Vanessa had seemed about perfect for him, except instead of fire between them, there hadn't even been ignition.

Not being jealous was one thing. But when they were in camp during those rare quiet moments of the busy fire season, Mickey paid much more attention to Robin than to his old still-single pal. Gordon supposed it only made sense, but he was all the happier about finding a friend in Vanessa to fill that unexpected void.

Up over the fire, they headed for their respective targets.

The real battle, the make-or-break on the fire, was going to happen in the next thirty minutes. Gordon checked his fuel. Yes, he'd be good for that long and Vanessa would be back in another ten.

The wildfire would soon be slamming up against the fire break that the smokies had punched through the trees. Flames were climbing two hundred feet into the air in a thick pall of smoke gone dark gray with all of the ash that the heat was carrying aloft.

With a single load, Gordon managed to hit three separate flare-ups behind the smokies' line. He could see the soot-stained smokie team below, clearing brush and scraping soil by hand even though the main flames were less than a hundred feet away. They had inch-and-a-half hoses charged up and were spraying down their own line.

Gordon swung for the lake, climbed through the smoke, and dove—

Something slammed into his windshield straight in front of his face.

He flinched and jerked.

Wrong shape and color for a bird.

Mechanical!

A hobby drone. A big one. Four rotors and a camera.

It star-cracked his acrylic windshield, then slid upward.

He didn't have a moment to plead with the fates before he felt his MD jolt.

Perfect—the drone slid straight into his engine's air intake.

Not a chance that his Allison 250 turboshaft engine would just chew up the plastic and spit it out the exhaust. Even if it did, the battery was like throwing a brick into the turbine.

The primary compressor, spinning at fifty thousand RPM, choked on the three-pound drone.

A horrendous grinding noise sounded close above his head.

Red lights flared, starting with "Engine Out" at the upper left of his console and a high warning tone in his headset.

Other indicators flared to life, but he ignored them. With the engine failed, nothing else really mattered.

Gordon eased down on the collective and twisted the throttle to the fuel cutoff position. The grinding sound slowed but grew rapidly worse—his engine wasn't just dead, it was shredding itself. He slammed a foot on the right pedal as the nose torqued to the left.

"Mayday! Mayday! Mayday!" At least he still had electrical power to the radios. "Hobby drone strike, straight into my engine. Going down."

The radio fired up with questions, but Gordon was in the death zone and didn't have time to listen. A lift-failure emergency in a helicopter below fifty feet or over four hundred was generally survivable. The range in between those two altitudes cut life expectancy a lot more than he wanted to think about at the moment. He was currently in heavy smoke, descending down through the one-fifty mark.

It was little comfort knowing that the FAA would slap the drone owner's wrist if they could find him. Of course, if this went as badly as Gordon was expecting, MHA would go after the asshole for a million-dollar helo and the cost of one funeral.

"God damn it! And I was in such a good mood." There, that sounded more like Vin Diesel than Austin Powers. Truly sad—he was going to have to die to get it right. Though he couldn't place what movie the line was from.

The smoke wrapped around him and visibility left altogether. He fought for best auto-rotate speed, but at the rate he was falling, there wasn't a whole lot of time to get there.

He'd started flying fifteen years ago on his family's ranch, spent the last three years with MHA, and this was his first real-life crash landing. All the practice in the world didn't count for shit.

His palms were sweating against the slick plastic of the controls. The cabin was filling with smoke, but he couldn't take his hands off the controls to close the vent to the outside.

With his right shoulder, he nudged up the

release lever on the pilot-side door. It swung open two inches and stabilized just like it was supposed to. The additional airflow helped the smoke flow through the cabin faster, but it still burnt his eyes and his throat. As a firefighter, he supposed that it was no surprise that death smelled like hot wood smoke.

His visibility was under twenty feet, and the smoke was taking on a distinctly orange glow. At sixty miles an hour, that gave him absolutely no lead time for maneuvering.

He wrestled east for the water.

The first treetop that slapped against his windshield was brilliant orange with flame. Lodgepole pine.

The next one, Douglas fir, snagged his left skid, jerking him sharply to the side before he was past it. If the one that slammed into his right-side pilot's window, white fir, made him scream, he didn't have time to realize it.

The next one, too buried in flames to recognize, ripped the door off entirely.

Gordon's instincts did what they could, with the controls now gone useless. One tree after another battered his helo: Ponderosa, western juniper—he ricocheted off the side of a massive Doug fir harder than being tossed by a bucking bronc.

The ends of rotor blades snapped off.

Then more of them.

The other skid snagged and twisted him the other direction, which saved him from the next flaming tree coming in through the missing door and killing him.

He realized that he was falling, treetop to treetop, down the steep bank toward the water.

His broken helicopter smashed through the last of the flaming line in a slow tumble thirty feet above the water.

With one final effort, he stomped on the right pedal and shoved the cyclic left.

No rotors. No effect.

That's when he remembered where the movie line was from. It wasn't Vin Diesel at all. It was John Goodman playing the hapless Al Yackey in the firefighting movie *Always.*

"No offense, John," he spoke his final words aloud to his dead helicopter. "But I'd rather die as Vin Diesel."

He plunged into the water upside down.

* * *

Five minutes earlier, Ripley Vaughan flew into sight of the firefight and eased her Erickson Aircrane to a hover.

"Wow!" "That's a mess!" Brad and Janet White, her married copilot and crew chief, did one of their synchro-speaking things.

They were right. It was.

The Black, the area already burned by the wildfire, ranged across five hundred acres. No cleanup had been done, there were spot fires dotted all over the Black, and the fire's flanks were eating sideways into the trees in addition to the main head of the fire driving toward a community. It could be the textbook definition of zero percent contained.

Ripley could see the hard slash of a smokejumper defense line across the rugged hills, cleared of trees and brush. It looked so small against the towering wall of fire bearing down on them, but then it always did from altitude. And there was a heavy airshow going on. The battle of this wildfire was about to be engaged big time.

They needed help. But without a contract, she wouldn't be insured *or* paid if she fought on this fire…unless.

"Are those aircraft painted black?"

Brad pulled out a small pair of binoculars. "Yep! With flames and all."

That meant it was Mount Hood Aviation, their new outfit.

Ripley watched the airshow for another thirty seconds and could see the smooth coordination of the attack effort. She'd been flying her big Aircrane helicopter to fire for a couple of years, but had never imagined she'd get the chance to fly for Mount Hood Aviation. They had the best reputation in the business. Their for-hire smokejumping team was right on par with the Forest Service's Missoula, Montana Zulies, but *nobody* had the renown of their helicopter team.

Back at Erickson's Medford airfield in southern Oregon, Randy had called her into his office.

"I've got a rest-of-season contract request here."

Ripley hadn't particularly cared where she went, as long as it kept her flying.

"For some reason, it came through with your name on it. Something going on here I don't know about?" He sounded some kinda pissed about it. Upsetting a chief pilot with his years of experience was never a good idea—especially not when he signed her paychecks. Randy's cheerful demeanor and the easy smile that normally showed through his white beard were completely missing. Now she could see a flash of that kick-ass retired Army Chief Warrant that was typically hidden away. Word was that he'd graduated top of his Army flight class and hadn't slowed down for an instant during his years with the 2/10 Air Cav, not that the stories ever came from him.

"Unless it's for dancing," Ripley eyed the paperwork Randy was waving at her, "I can't imagine why it would be for me."

With her crew being named Brad and Janet—and Janet looking like a young Susan Sarandon, it was inevitable that their crew would learn "The Time Warp" dance from *The Rocky Horror Picture Show*…and then get known for it. But she hadn't been shopping for someplace else to be; she liked flying for Erickson more than she had liked anything else since she'd left the Navy.

Randy had tossed over the paperwork and Ripley had glanced down at it. She didn't spot her name anywhere. It was a contract for "your best pilot" from Mount Hood Aviation.

His scowl changed to his usual cheery smile. "Man's gotta have some fun. A couple pilots here are as good as you, but I don't have any that are better. You want to fly with MHA for what's left of the season, it's yours. You've earned it. But…" and he'd aimed a finger out toward the landing apron where her helicopter baked under the Medford late-summer heat. That former-military voice came out again, "You better bring my bird back in one piece. Yourself too, while you're at it."

She'd promised she would and then signed it on the spot. It was only later that she thought to ask Brad and Janet, but they were game as always.

The three of them with their Aircrane were supposed to be transiting to MHA's base today but now had stumbled on their new outfit in a full-on firefight.

"Janet, let's scoop up some water. Brad, find me this fire's Air Attack frequency because I can't fly into a restricted Fire Traffic Area without permission."

There was a lake down below that she

could see the other helos were using. It was just long enough that she could use the sea snorkel instead of the pond snorkel. The latter would require hovering and pumping. The sea snorkel was designed to let her fill her tanks on the fly. She could lower the snorkel's long strut to drag the tip below the surface and use the force of her own flying speed to fill the tanks. It was much quicker.

She flew down over the south end of Rock Creek Reservoir.

"Snorkel in five," she called out. Ripley could run the controls from her left side command seat, but since she had her crew chief aboard for the transit, Ripley let her have something to do. Her real duties would be on the ground once they arrived, but it was a chance for Janet to get a little control time in her log book.

"In five," Janet called back. She sat in the observer's seat directly behind Ripley, facing backward. That seat was positioned so that a pilot could control the helo during finicky winching jobs, like when they were assembling transmission towers. Not really needed for firefighting, but it gave her crew chief somewhere to sit and be a part of the firefight.

Ripley flew down until her big helo's wheels were just ten feet above the water. Once they slowed to thirty knots, Janet lowered the sea snorkel's strut into the water. Their speed alone would cause the water to shoot into the two submerged openings on the pipe, each the size of her palm. The water would blow upward like a thirty-five-mile-an-hour firehose. In forty seconds and just over half a mile, they could load up twenty-five hundred gallons of water, a dozen large hot tubs' worth, and be heading for the fire.

She flew along the line of the burning shore as it curved around from east to north. Rock Creek entered at the northern tip of the reservoir, providing her with an excellent gap in the trees for her climb out.

Brad found the frequency.

MHA's communications blasted into Ripley's headset.

"Did anyone see where he went down?" The voice was nearly frantic.

"All aircraft," a powerful male voice called out over the airwaves. "Climb and pull back. There was a civilian drone over the fire. It's already taken out one of our birds, we don't want to lose another. We need to evacuate. Keep an eye out for Gordon, but continue retreat."

Ripley had been on a number of fires where all of the air attack—helicopters, fixed-wing tankers, and command aircraft—had to pull back because someone had spotted a stupid civilian drone. There wasn't a firefighter aloft who hadn't thought about the dangers. But…

Ripley pressed the button on the back of the cyclic control with the tip of her index finger and transmitted. "If it already hit someone, then it's out of the sky. The chances of two simultaneous idiots on the same fire seems pretty low."

"Identify!" The ICA snapped out the command.

"This is Erickson Aircrane *Diana*—Oh shit!"

Ripley saw the body floating directly in her path. It was too late to avoid by climbing or raising the sea snorkel's strut.

* * *

Gordon had been floating on his back, watching the sky. It was amazing how pretty the sky was when you'd suddenly been given a reprieve from certain death. Even the fire still raging along the shore was a wonder of smoke and light as it swirled aloft.

He wanted to feel sad about the loss of his helo, but it was hard. His MD 530 had seen him through hell and given its own life to save his. He'd managed to release his seat harness and swim free before the helo hit the bottom of the reservoir. That first breath of air had been so clear and so sharp that he'd never forget it, not for as long as he lived.

A low thrumming echoed through the water, a heavy bass beat that only a helicopter could create, a big one like a Firehawk.

He opened his eyes and lifted his head to see if they'd come for him.

From less than a hundred feet away, he looked straight into the face of a beautiful helicopter pilot.

If there were moments he was never going to forget, the next three seconds were clogged with them.

The pilot sat almost fully exposed by the curved windshield of the helicopter. Gorgeous. Her straight black hair fell past her shoulders.

Her skin was the color of mid-roast coffee with just that perfect amount of cream. Her dark glasses and pilot's helmet with mic boom added to the image. Hot professional female pilot.

The next impression was how huge the approaching helicopter was—and because it was so close, it seemed twice its normal size. Instead of the vicious sleekness of a Black Hawk, it had a bulbous nose and was brilliant orange like the Muppet Beaker, who always looked as alarmed as Gordon was starting to feel.

The last impression, more memorable than anything else—except perhaps that knock-out pilot now looking almost directly down at him—was the long white boom that the Aircrane was slicing through the water.

Straight toward him!

There wasn't time to react. Hell, there wasn't even time to blink.

Gordon braced himself to be chopped in two.

Available at fine retailers everywhere.

Other works by M.L. Buchman

The Night Stalkers

Main Flight

The Night Is Mine
I Own the Dawn
Wait Until Dark
Take Over at Midnight
Light Up the Night
Bring On the Dusk
By Break of Day

White House Holiday

Daniel's Christmas
Frank's Independence Day
Peter's Christmas
Zachary's Christmas
Roy's Independence Day
Cornelia's Christmas

and the Navy

Christmas at Steel Beach
Christmas at Peleliu Cove

5E

Target of the Heart
Target Lock on Love

Firehawks

Main Flight

Pure Heat
Full Blaze
Hot Point

Flash of Fire
Wild Fire

Smokejumpers
Wildfire at Dawn
Wildfire at Larch Creek
Wildfire on the Skagit

Delta Force
Target Engaged
Heart Strike

Angelo's Hearth
Where Dreams are Born
Where Dreams Reside
Maria's Christmas Table
Where Dreams Unfold
Where Dreams Are Written

Eagle Cove
Return to Eagle Cove
Recipe for Eagle Cove
Longing for Eagle Cove
Keepsake for Eagle Cove

Deities Anonymous
Cookbook from Hell: Reheated
Saviors 101

Dead Chef Thrillers
Swap Out!
One Chef!
Two Chef!

SF/F Titles

Nara
Monk's Maze
The Me and Elsie Chronicles

Get a free Starter Library at:
www.mlbuchman.com

20637716R00052

Printed in Great Britain
by Amazon